Rocking the CEO

A 1Night Stand Story

By
Catherine Peace

Copyright © 2016 by Catherine Peace
ISBN: 978-1-68361-096-0
Cover art by Mina Carter

Published by
Decadent Publishing Company, LLC

Look for us online at:
www.decadentpublishing.com

~A Note from the Author~

When I wrote *Complete Me* two years ago, I was going through a difficult time where another woman was the antagonist of my relationship (which is a whole long story in itself.) But since I got away from that entire fiasco, I realized just how much we put women in competition with other women, in writing or in life, and I made the conscious decision to pull Joss away from that and give her a second chance at life and at love instead of letting her remain a two-dimensional villain.

The purpose of romance is to give everyone a chance at a Happily Ever After. Even the ones who may seem unlovable at first, or conceited, or lost. Like many, Joss was broken, afraid of being alone, and scared of her own potential. How many people do we know like that? How many do we write off? I wanted to give Joss this chance because she deserves it.

And so do you.

Sincerely,
Catherine Peace

If you like what you read, drop me a line at c.peace@live.com!

Dedication

To anyone who's ever needed a second chance.

Acknowledgements

Thanks to Connie Smith for, once again, lending her genius song lyrics to my book. You're a rock star!

Chapter One

*H*oly shit. Joss stared, mouth hung open, certain her eyes deceived her. In the harsh Nevada sun, Sin City filled her vision with signs guaranteeing riches and pleasure and so many promises, promises, promises. "We made it," she whispered.

Reaching for a strand of hair to twirl, her nervous habit, she brushed her shoulder instead, thanks to the bright-red pixie cut she kept forgetting about—part of Rachel's "New You" campaign, which so far included a move to the West Coast, a new wardrobe, and a new drummer for their band, Valkyrie Rysing. She adored the fun-sized, she-beast Pippa, a bubbly blonde whose kit almost swallowed her whole, and who blew Joss's mind at the audition. Most men didn't have the balls to play like Pippa Wallace.

It'd taken a lot to get Joss to this point, mostly her breakup with Anderson almost a year ago. But the band got into clubs and bars around L.A. with their music, not with her daddy's connections, which equaled a dream come true, the first she remembered in a long time.

"Sin City!" Pip pumped her fist in the air. "I can't believe we're *here*!"

"Me neither."

When the drummer had brought up the Las Vegas contest for a contract with ICE Records, it'd been in jest. And then it'd moved into a "why not?" sort of thing, which led to cutting an actual demo in Rachel's studio and sending the demo in with the lowest of low expectations.

Considering they got in without her father's pull, Joss thought maybe they were good enough. All her life, she'd depended on him and the connections he made while touring with Springsteen. A killer guitar player, he stayed modest, content to hang in the back and let Bruce have all the fun. Too bad she hadn't gotten his disdain for the spotlight; maybe her relationships would've lasted longer.

"We've got tonight to play tourist. Tomorrow, though, we gotta focus," Rachel said.

"All work and no play...." Joss elbowed her friend.

"Oh, well, *one* of us'll be getting some play." The bassist got a wicked grin on her face, the one that made Joss wonder if the band name shouldn't have been *Devil Rysing*. "I have a little surprise for you."

Joss rolled her eyes. "I feel like I'm on *Oprah*."

"Okay, Oprah? Not rock 'n roll, dear. Not at all."

"Sorry, but nothing rock-approved comes with so many damn surprises. Well, good ones, anyway. New home, new style, new clothes? What's next?"

"Pippa!"

Turning to peek in the backseat, Joss caught a view of their drummer she did *not* want. "Oh my God, you cannot flash the other cars. Put the girls away, please and thank you."

With a groan, she complied. "You guys are no fun."

"We'd like to *get* to the competition, not miss it because you can't keep your damn shirt on. At least wait till we're at the hotel, okay?"

Once the ruckus in the SUV calmed down, she pondered what Rachel's surprise might be but refused bring it up again. Part of her didn't want to ask.

About half an hour later, they settled into their room. "Good thing your dad's loaded," Joss said.

"Yeah. He comes in handy. Trying to buy my love all the time." Rachel flopped on the bed and crossed her ankles. "He's how I got my sweet-ass Gibson Firebird."

"Which you haven't taken out of the case yet." Joss glanced around the suite. Bright-white duvets covered the two queen-sized beds. A silver-gray wingback chair took up one corner, and an ornate, walnut-stained desk sat against the wall opposite the beds. Roomy, comfortable, luxurious...bright. "Martha Stewart decorate this?"

"I like it," Pippa said. "There's nothing wrong with some light, Vampire Queen."

"I guess you're right, Pipsqueak."

Meanwhile, Rachel flailed around like a kid at a rave while trying to fish something out of her pocket. Succeeding, she unfolded the itinerary the contest coordinators had provided. "Says we need to get our gear to the venue by seven tonight."

"Might as well get it over with now. Then we can come back and decide what we want to do." Joss picked up the hotel information guide. "Oooh, room service."

"Keep flipping, doll. You'll see the reason we're staying here," Rachel said.

She did. Close to the back, a list of nightclubs with accompanying photos and descriptions whet her appetite. "Rendezvous?"

"Hottest club in the city, right here in our hotel. The Castillos equal party kings." Sitting up, Rachel flashed her wicked smile again. "That, my dear, is where you'll be meeting your date."

"My *what*?"

Running her hands through her choppy hair, she said, "I, uh, got you a date," with as much enthusiasm as a hungover frat boy after a bender.

Record scratch. "No."

"Yes. Through the 1Night Stand thing." Under Joss's glare, the bassist wilted. She pulled her knees against her chest as though they'd protect her from the verbal beat down formulating in Jocelyn's mind like a hurricane. "I found a coupon."

"I can't believe you! That fucking site wrecked my life."

"Noooooo, it released you. You deserve way better than what you've gotten."

Did she? She'd tormented Ty for a decade, often behind the back of a man she thought she loved. At twenty-nine, she'd developed a different definition of better—more music, less drama. Considering the strain this whole *emotion* BS added, she gave up on love to concentrate on songwriting, performing, crafting a signature vocal style. In her experience, with her parents' divorce and her break up with Anderson, love and happiness only mixed in melody, not real life. "I already told you. I want to focus on the band."

Rachel shook her head. "Sweetheart, if I can be honest, you've been bitchy as hell since you stopped getting laid."

"Hmph."

"Pip and I are worried about you, that's all, babe."

The drummer nodded enthusiastically and then turned her attention back to their, admittedly breathtaking view of the Strip.

"You need to be worried about the band, not my sex life."

"Okay, then how about this?" Rachel unfurled and crossed her arms over her chest. "Your songwriting has gone to shit."

"Wow. Hit me right where it hurts, Rach."

"Can't help it. You suck now."

She'd figured that a long time ago, but hearing it? No, thank you. "Fuck you very much." So what? She'd hit a slump. "Clapton hit slumps from time to time," Dad told her once. Freaking *Clapton*. "I'm...in a tough space."

"Yeah, and maybe getting some action will grease the wheels, so to speak."

"You're awful. And as sex obsessed as a teenage boy."

"I make no apologies for the way my brain works."

Ugh. Suddenly, the idea of clubs no longer appealed. "I'm not doing it."

"Too late, babe. I told him you'd be there." Rachel's stone-set face spoke volumes on her resolve.

I'm not getting out of this. "When?"

"Sunday night. At Rendezvous."

Oh. My. God. The fucking competition's after-party? Seriously? "I...I need some damn air." Quick as lightning, Joss grabbed her purse and headed for destination unknown.

Chapter Two

August Bragg stared into his drink. The sounds of the club bled into the hallway, into his ears, and he tapped his foot to the rhythm. Music always gave him the urge to move, as though the sound tickled him. Maybe it did.

Mentally, he ticked off the seconds until Saturday night's competition. Tomorrow night, the bands would have to practice—complete with sound checks, lighting consultations, everything to ensure perfection. Then Saturday…. His blood thrummed with the promise of fresh music for his label, his ears, his soul.

ICE Records boasted some of the hottest new bands in the country, with their unique sounds getting significant airtime on the radio, hitting the top of the Billboard charts, selling out arenas left and right, and headlining festivals.

He'd found those bands through competitions like the one this weekend, and, from the demos he'd already heard, he anticipated a tough decision. Would the live sound hold up, or were the recordings products of studio magic? Raw sound with some rough edges he and Micah understood and helped refine every year. Studio magic? A crowd would eat those musicians alive.

He drained his glass then motioned to his favorite bartender for another Deveraux, a drink only Danny got right. The older man possessed a disarming demeanor, and, considering August's appearance—the piercings and visible tattoos, which sometimes caused people on the street to move away from him—he appreciated Danny's ability to treat him like a normal person. Not like a tatted, pierced thug or like the owner of a record label producing serious talent year after year. No, these conversations provided the sense of normalcy August got the Friday before the competition, when his favorite bartender made his favorite drink.

"How's this year lookin' for ya?" he asked in his musical Irish voice.

August smiled. Leave it to Danny to remember why he came to Vegas, though, with his appearance, he expected to be unforgettable. "Better than ever. There are some amazing bands coming in this weekend. I might have trouble choosing."

"Any front-runners?"

Always a loaded question. Policy dictated he say no, so people thought him unbiased. "A couple," he admitted. "I've been praying for the sound to hold up live."

"Very good."

Very good, indeed. Two captured his hopes: Black Water and Valkyrie Rysing. Especially the second one. The lead singer's voice had given him both chills *and* an erection, and he prayed her voice would sound as strong, as deep, and as sensual—or better—on Saturday. *One more day....* His cock twitched at the thought while Natalia Bishop's voice resonated in his mind. Since listening to their demo a few months ago, he'd fantasized about her, imagining the face that went along with that stunning voice. As a rule, he prohibited bands from sending photos to avoid creating a bias. ICE Records valued music first, image second.

For the first time in four years, he regretted that rule.

"I'm pretty stoked," he said to the bartender. "Pretty damn stoked."

Out of the corner of his eye, August spotted a flash of bright red, and the rest of his attention followed his gaze. His heart nearly stopped, and, before he thought about it, he abandoned his half-finished Devereaux. She drew him like music drew him, an embodiment of the goddess Freyja down to her red hair. *Natalia?*

The woman headed toward Rendezvous, one of the best clubs in Vegas and one of his favorite places to go. With the way they were dressed, neither of them would be allowed in, but he wanted her name. No, he *needed* it.

She stopped at the entrance and leaned against the wall. With her spiked hair, tight black T-shirt, the swell of her ass in those black skinny jeans, and spike-heeled boots, she personified his fantasy. How could he focus on his date Sunday night when this woman stood in front of him, the picture of everything he'd wanted for months?

He stopped next to her and tried not to stare, but her beauty captivated him. Bright-green eyes, a narrow nose, and a gorgeous mouth he wanted to taste so badly he barely withstood being next to her. *Keep your composure. She's a woman. A beautiful woman….* "Hello there."

When she glanced at him, her eyes widened just a bit. "Hi." Then she curled her lips into a seductive smile.

"You look a little lost."

She shrugged. "Hard to be lost when you don't have a destination."

Gods, her voice…. Pure, raw, Southern sex appeal. "Where are you from?"

"South Carolina. You?"

"Iceland." He appreciated the interest in her eyes and the way she pursed her lips.

"Your accent's sexy."

"So is yours."

At the compliment, she actually blushed. "Thank you."

"You're welcome." Shouting over the music started to get old. "Would you like to go somewhere?"

From the way her green eyes darkened, he knew her answer before she said a word.

No way they'd make it back to his room, not with the way he ached. Time for an alternative plan.

Chapter Three

*H*oly shit—no other words existed. Beneath the leather jacket he wore, she suspected him to be solid muscle. Plenty of rocker guys were unassuming like this, and she'd learned how to tell. This guy? *Oh, yeah.* He'd have muscles she'd want her tongue on. Soon.

All at once, her engines revved. Maybe the accent set it off. Maybe his general hotness—the eyebrow ring, nose ring, the symbol tattoo on his neck, the short and spiky brown hair that highlighted his sky-blue eyes. Regardless, her sex drive jumped into warp speed.

And with the way her body pulsated, she wouldn't be able to wait to get in a room, hers or otherwise, roommates be damned.

Jesus, she didn't even know his name.

Fuck it.

Whether he meant go somewhere else to talk or not, she pressed her body against his and snaked her tongue into his mouth before she took the time to parse his question. He tasted like sweet whiskey and man and everything that made her pussy ache. His hands cupped her ass and pressed her pelvis into his erection, and her breath caught. How long had it been? Well over a year. She and Anderson had stopped having sex long before their inevitable end.

Don't give him headspace. He doesn't matter anymore.

Her new friend broke away from her and grabbed her hand. Chest heaving, she followed him from the club toward the registration desk. Then he made a sudden turn down a side hallway leading to...the restrooms.

She smiled.

No stupid date required to get her mojo back. No 1Night Stand or interference from Rachel. This man *wanted* her, desired her. What else did she need?

They entered the empty men's room. Limited options. One stall. With a wink, he pulled her into the stall and locked the door. In the next second, he covered her mouth with his, hands roving everywhere, up her sides to her breasts, to her back, her ass, her thighs. Everywhere she'd ached to be touched for so long. The throbbing between her legs cranked up to eleven. She tugged at the fly of his jeans and broke from his lips, which immediately went to her jaw and then to her neck.

"Please tell me you have protection," she whispered.

Rather than answer, he reached into his back pocket and pulled out his wallet. He cursed in an unfamiliar language—Icelandic, she figured—and fished the condom out. With the break, she opened his jeans and wrapped her fingers around his swollen cock. *God almighty.*

He groaned at the contact, an almost animalistic

sound that went straight between her legs. With shaking hands, he opened the wrapper and slid the condom on. Then he kissed her again, fingers working at the buttons on her jeans, and the biggest relief ever washed over her when he pushed her pants and panties down her hips. He slipped two long fingers inside her, and she shivered with the deliciousness of the pressure. Mumbling in his beautiful language again, he removed his fingers and entered her.

"Oh, *fuck*," she moaned, burying her head in his shoulder. She slid his jacket off his shoulders, satisfied by the *fwomp* of it hitting the floor. Then she searched for whatever bare skin she could find while sweet, sweet fullness, completeness overwhelmed her, searing the broken spots of her soul closed for a little while. Nails biting into his shoulders, she tried to muffle her cry, but people outside probably heard her anyway.

While he finished, her orgasm still rippled through her, leaving her in a headspace of pure Zen—something she hadn't experienced since long before she and Anderson split. The same headspace that allowed her to forget all the bullshit around her and write kick-ass lyrics. *Wonder if Rach can get her money back?*

For a few moments, August's mind was perfectly blank, devoid of the thoughts often swirling around nonstop. He didn't obsess over the competition, or fear the failure his father had promised him, or panic about not signing a new band. Once they parted, however, he'd return to the over thinking and over analyzing that made him one of the shrewdest CEOs in the business.

Then a song he'd heard a million times on the radio broke his sense of peace. "'Beautiful Blaze,'" he muttered.

"Shit. Yeah. I keep meaning to change that...."

He disengaged from her and, suddenly embarrassed, resituated himself and stepped back while she did the same. Reaching into her back pocket, she retrieved her cell phone and cursed as she answered. "Hi, Pipsqueak.... Yeah, I'm okay. I know, I know. I'm on my way." She hung up. "I'm sorry. I've gotta go."

"Sure, sure." Throat dry, he glanced everywhere but at her.

She fumbled for the stall lock. "So um...yeah. Thanks for that," she said with a nervous chuckle.

"My pleasure," he replied. Not at all a lie. "May I at least have your name?"

She nodded. "Joss." Then she left.

I suppose I'll be keeping my date after all.

Chapter Four

By the next day, Joss's body still thrummed from her Icelandic dreamboat's touch, his lips and hands. Her ears still rang with his sultry voice, and her brain still berated her for not getting his name. Stupid. A guy that freaking hot was a guy whose name you asked for. Cardinal rule. And she broke it.

Last night, she'd gone through the motions of unloading and storing the gear, unconcerned with the thumping and bumping of the guitar cases. Her mind still reeled with what'd taken place. Vegas was a big enough city that her odds of seeing him again were worse than a gambling addict's odds of leaving the table on a hot streak. Nil, none, bad all the way around.

And, of course, she'd gotten the requisite tongue-lashing from Rachel. How *dare* she do something so juvenile? As bad as Pip's flashing other cars had been, this amounted to a capital offense. Sex with a stranger in a public restroom registered as Defcon One on Rach's List of Terrible Ideas. Especially since it could've gotten them all booted from the hotel.

And somewhere in the back of her mind where logic still existed, Joss understood most of that. But at the time, she'd lacked the wherewithal to be concerned.

Unpacking her gear, she worried about her bassist's cold shoulder dampening their performance. The show depended on their back-and-forth call and answers, their chemistry, their mutual love for music. Without her playing along, embracing the music and the electricity around them, Valkyrie Rysing would only rise right back to Los Angeles. No contract. No future.

Dammit, she *would* have a future.

While Pippa set up her monster kit, Joss pulled Rachel aside. "We okay?"

"Yeah. I'm still kinda pissed at you, though." She slid her fingers down the neck of her bass. "I really cannot believe you did that."

"It was stupid. I know. Won't happen again."

"Good." She turned away to plug her cord into the amp. "We have to get this right. I'm not going back to L.A. a loser."

"Neither am I. I'm ready. We got this." Joss knew it to her bones.

On the info sheet, the record company warned that their VP attended the sound checks, and first impressions determined who moved on to Saturday night's live performance round. Glancing around the empty venue, she spotted an older man in a light-gray suit, handsome in a completely un-rock-like sort of way. Hell, from the stage, Joss shivered from the authoritative air resonating like a deep bass note, and, with his shrewd gaze, he pushed that disappointed-parent button, like he'd spent a fortune on guitar lessons just for his kid to decide to play football instead.

All right, then. Time to knock Micah Davis's socks off.

Natalia. The red-haired spitfire he'd been unable to resist. Gods above, what had he done?

He'd become biased, the exact thing he'd always avoided.

Steeling himself and returning to a state of calm, August stayed away from the line of the stage and let Micah take the reins. The night before, he'd managed maybe a couple hours' sleep, and, when he faded into dreams, he kept envisioning her, hearing her breathy moans and sighs, the voice he tried desperately to forget. But Freyja had blessed this fire-haired woman, filling her music with magic enough to beguile him, even into his deepest fantasies.

After a few moments, Joss started running her fingers up the neck of her guitar. The honey-toned notes of a warm-up filled the air, and the room already buzzed. When the bassist, Rachel Mathers, joined in, he closed his eyes, unwilling to look at Joss and yet unable to resist the pull of the music they created. What began as a simple riff grew into a lullaby, and once Pippa Jameson added her easy cadence, the music carried him to a distant place he hadn't seen in a long while, thanks to an overbearing family who disowned him for following his passion.

Then it ended. Opening his eyes, he watched Joss and Rachel confer. Then Joss spoke into the mic. "Can we get a little more guitar in the bass monitor, please?"

A simple request that got him rock-hard in a matter of seconds, regardless of the fact she spoke to Jake, the sound tech, and not to him. The older man upped the guitar until Rachel nodded, and then made a note on his scratch pad, no doubt writing down the band's preferred sound levels. He made the necessary adjustments for each of them.

A familiar bass riff pounded from the speakers, followed by Pippa's staccato hits on the hi-hat. One-and-two-and-three-and-four-and.... "Soulless," one of their demo songs. Swallowing hard, he anticipated Natalia's—Joss's—growling vocals.

It wasn't love that blinded me
It was the darkness you radiate
Leave me drowning and subsiding
In naked lies that you create

Till I am covered in the thickest veil
Shielding me from a sign of hope
Strands of faith are growing pale
In the darkness of your blackened soul

I don't require an alibi
I don't desire your condolence
Gaze into reflective eyes
Realize that you are soulless
Burning wrath, no compromise
That rebukes the slightest solace
A hardened heart left petrified
From shadowed love, dark and soulless

The keeper of everything empty and grave
Lost and confused, tortured and torn

Enclosed entrance to this maze
Keeps new dreams from being born

She tore into the chorus again like a wild animal, her voice raw and full of emotion, then into the next bridge with a whisper that made his heart jump.

Trapped deep within this quiet stillness
As agony echoes against its walls
No light of hope to be my witness
To answer my most desperate calls

She went through the chorus one last time. *Holy shit.* Her range...how she kept an audience, Micah Davis and battle-tested sound guys enraptured.... He glanced at his right-hand man, the only ear he trusted besides his own. The man's wide eyes and open mouth said it all.

Valkyrie Rysing had one hell of a chance.

Better than a chance. He'd heard most of the bands already, and to him, they were the front runners, meaning they'd get the prime-time spot at the competition unless someone else knocked them out of it. Black Water needed to be nothing short of perfect to accomplish that.

"Mark them down for the 10:00 p.m. slot. For now," he added. "Though I don't know who might top that."

Micah nodded. "You sure we even *need* the next two nights? That? Was a sound check. A fucking *sound check,* and they killed it. Pete's jaw is still on the floor."

True. He ached to sign them on the spot, but their protocol existed for a reason. "Let's make sure they don't fall apart under pressure." Though he'd already experienced how Joss handled pressure…. "Make your introductions. Give me your feedback. I'm anxious to see how well they do tomorrow."

"Yes, sir."

Chapter Five

"I don't think I've ever celebrated a sound check before." Pippa downed her butterscotch shot like a pro.

Micah Davis's glowing review gave them a fantastic reason to celebrate. The veep threw words like "bold," "magical," and "daring" like a beach ball at a Jack Johnson show. Best of all, they landed the 10:00 p.m. slot for the first night of the competition.

Slamming the shot glass back onto the bar, Joss grinned. "One's never been this important. 'Sides, this is step one, ladies."

"More shots!"

Rachel laughed. "Yes, Pip. More shots."

For being such a tiny thing, the girl held her liquor. Joss already enjoyed a nice buzz, but more booze threatened to leave her voice shot for tomorrow night. "Water for me, please. Gotta save the ol' vocal chords."

The girls acquiesced. Then ordered more shots.

"You can put those on our tab."

Oh, fuck my life. She didn't have to turn around to know who stood behind her. Blake Young, hot-as-hell lead singer for Black Water. No doubt Dominik, the drummer, checked out her ass, like he always did when they were in the same zip code. "Trying to soften up the competition, Blake?"

His breathy chuckle sounded at her ear. Rather than entice, it raised her hackles. She'd seen the band before, on a trip to New Orleans with Dad, who'd been good friends with Dominik's father. Most days, she barely tolerated her own father, but his faults paled in comparison to the Lamberts'. Like creepy, misogynistic father, like creepy, misogynistic son.

But she still preferred him to the grade-A douche standing way too close to her for comfort. A chiseled face, forest-green eyes, and curly shoulder-length black hair—sex hair, as Rachel called it—only served to hide the hideous soul underneath.

"Trying to be friendly, *chère*. Nothing more."

"For Christ's sake, you can cut the Bayou Don Juan act. Fish ain't biting over here."

"I might," Pip said.

Lord. No way to deal with this right now. "I wouldn't if I were you. No telling where it's been."

He scoffed. "You think you even got a chance this weekend?" Ah, much better. Less Johnny Depp in *Chocolat*, more typical Southern redneck asshole.

"I do." She whirled around to see his reaction to her next statement. "So does Micah Davis. Last I checked, he called the shots. Not you."

Blake's handsome face turned smug. He leaned in, much closer than Joss would *ever* prefer. "Little girls don't belong in rock. You'll figure that out the hard way."

At that moment, she thought she could breathe fire. Too bad the fuckers she wanted to roast were already gone.

"No more shots, ladies," she said. "We've got some work to do."

***

In the end, Black Water won Micah over, so they added an 11:00 p.m. spot to the show. As he'd said, they sounded like sweet molasses dripping over a honeycomb. Not something August knew, but he trusted his VP enough to include seven bands instead of the normal six. The expo board displayed band names and times, but his attention kept coming back to Valkyrie Rysing, sandwiched between Black Water and Agave.

"Give me your thoughts," he said.

Micah leaned back in his chair, loosened his tie. "I know who my top three would be. The sound checks were some of the best we've heard, and there were some sleepers who sound better live than on their demos."

"Agreed." After listening to Joss, he'd left Micah for that much-needed alone time. "Give me the rundown."

The other man went down the list of band names, giving generic feedback. Good sound, easygoing, impressive technique. When he reached Valkyrie Rysing, he said, "They're still my favorite, man, though I have no doubt Black Water will kill in front of an audience. Those ladies are marketable. Tough, sexy, and Natalia Bishop's voice is pure sex."

You've no idea. "So that was your O-face I saw?"

Micah's rich laughter filled the room. "Almost."

"Who is band number three, in your opinion?"

After a few minutes of staring at the board, the other man said, "Agave. They're out of the box, for sure. Did you hear them?"

He thought for a moment. "No. They played after Valkyrie."

"It's good stuff. Depeche Mode-style vocals against an industrial sound. Haunting."

"The name would have to change." Though he understood the significance of a plant whose flowers bloom once and then die, not everyone would. "We'll see if tomorrow night's audience shares your tastes."

"I haven't been wrong in four years."

Good point.

After Micah left, August stayed at the office to try to clear his mind. Last night had been such a mistake, and yet seeing Joss again failed to quell his desire for her, regardless of how poorly it reflected on him. He'd been with enough women to recognize the difference between lust and...more. Something sparked between them, the beginning of a new journey, whether either of them accepted it or not.

Tomorrow night, he'd introduce himself to the winners. Deep in his gut, he knew Joss would be waiting for him.

Chapter Six

The competition proved tighter than August anticipated. A couple of bands who hadn't impressed him during sound checks brought their A-game and drove the crowd nuts. Every few minutes, he checked his watch. The hands limped toward 10:00 p.m. His body, his soul, needed to see Joss in action.

By the time the appropriate hour rolled around, electricity and alcohol fueled the crowd, and their energy bled into him, demolishing his normal cool, calm, collected demeanor and replacing it with the spasmodic vigor of someone on a three-day coke bender. His entire body came alive at the simple thought of Valkyrie Rysing taking the stage and claiming their place in the finals.

Thus far, men dominated the stage. How would the audience react to a trio of beauties?

As Joss stepped onto the stage in a barely-there black miniskirt, ripped tights, and a sleeveless black shirt that showed off her toned arms, he got his answer.

They went wild.

She'd spiked her hair and applied a dark eye shadow that made her green eyes electric. Watching her checking her gear alone got him hard. He held no hope that he'd make it through this performance unscathed.

Or unbiased.

The bassist joined her then the drummer—he only knew because he heard their warm-ups—but he refused to take his eyes off her. The way she prowled the stage like she owned it turned him on more than anything. *Stay focused.* But his mind…. No. He lost this neutrality fight long before it began.

A power chord rumbled in the amp and Joss's snarl set his blood on fire. She grabbed the mic and surveyed the crowd. "Fuck yeah, Vegas!" she called. As expected, the already-rowdy crowd got rowdier. She grinned a feral, seductive grin. "You guys ready to get your eardrums rocked by three hot-ass chicks?" Then she scanned the room. And the moment she saw him, her eyes widened and her face fell.

The noise grew to a deafening roar.

Without any other introduction, the band lit into an unfamiliar song. Every single body in the room jumped to their feet, fists pumping, heads banging. August stood in the shadows and tapped his foot; more movement than that had the potential for either a deeply embarrassing moment in his pants or some kind of injury. His raging hard-on wasn't thwarted by Joss missing her lead-in to vocals. Twice. Thank God she recovered as gracefully as she did.

He forced himself into the neutral zone he'd occupied for the last several hours and studied the crowd reactions, the way the ladies carried themselves on stage, how they got people pumped for their music. Once the last strains of the song died, the screaming and clapping that followed almost forced him to cover his ears. More people pushed toward the stage, eager to get as close as possible to the trio. Glancing around for security, he found them already in place should there be a problem. While he loved rowdy shows, he hated riots.

The next chords brought his attention back to the stage, and he grinned. A version of Joan Jett's "I Love Rock 'n' Roll" filled the room with Rachel's hard bass drops and Pippa's intricate beats. Smart. The song lent itself to Joss's gritty vocals, and no doubt everyone remembered the lyrics, no matter how drunk they were. Sing-alongs were perfect for bands who weren't well-known.

Valkyrie Rysing's forty-five minutes passed too quickly. "Good night, you crazy fuckers!" Joss called to the roaring crowd. "You've made this ride a hell of a lot of fun for us, and we'd like to take a quick sec to thank ICE Records for giving us a shot." After blowing a kiss, she bounded offstage after her bandmates. Not until Black Water followed did the cheers and whistles die down.

Something like pride flowed through him. His body had already claimed her; seemed his heart was well on its way.

*****

She pretended she hadn't seen him. If she pretended, if she tried hard enough to forget then it'd never happened, right? And, not only had she *not* seen him, but she *definitely* hadn't seen him talking to Micah Davis. Nope, nope, nope. Totally a hallucination. Fever dream. Bad booze.

Not getting his name had bitten her in the ass. *Hard*.

A sweat-drenched towel smacked her in the face. Pip's wild laughter filled the backstage area, and the other five bands gawked at them with a mix of lust and confusion. As the only women in the middle of a sausage fest, they held everyone's attention. No leaving until Micah Davis chose the bands. After that, the three remaining would get some kind of speech from the CEO, August Bragg. More guys in suits. Exactly what they all wanted.

Seeing the VP of ICE Records chatting up Mr. Iceland meant absolutely nothing, right?

Joss grabbed a bottle of liquid denial and took a long, healthy swig. The 1Night Stand date danced in the back of her mind like a stripper desperate for a dollar. Too much longer in the background and it'd crawl to the forefront and demand the spotlight.

More beer. More beer right the fuck now.

Another drink of horse piss brought her back to the present.

Rachel tapped her shoulder and grabbed her wrist, dragging her to an unoccupied corner. Though she knew every eye in the room was on them simultaneously searching for a weakness and hoping for some girl-on-girl, she prepped herself for a healthy talking-to from her best friend.

"You all right? I've never heard you fuck up like that before."

She'd walked onto the stage all hardcore rock star, like she'd already been signed and the world bowed at her feet. Then she spotted *him* and Micah talking to him, and her entire world imploded. She'd missed her lead-in to "Rise," a song she sang in her sleep. At least she'd recovered. The suite probably realized she'd fucked up because their job required it.

"I'm fine. But...that guy I told you about? He's *here*." Conveniently, she left out the part where he and Micah Davis appeared to be besties.

Rachel stayed silent. She twisted a tendril of dreadlocked brown hair around her finger—her "contemplation stance."

Joss decided to head her off at the pass. "Look, I didn't expect it. Threw me off. A little. You have to admit we finished strong. Those people were practically clawing at each other to get to us."

Hah! Stumped. No recovery from that.

After a couple more beers, Joss's brain stopped whirling around. A nice buzz flowed through her system, and, for a few blessed minutes, she forgot Mr. Iceland was in the audience and that two of her least-favorite people on the planet were playing on stage. Their Southern-blues-rock sound worked in NOLA, but how would a Vegas crowd respond? Still, Black Water had some stiff competition in this room, like Agave, who'd shocked her to her boots. Good ol' hard rockers Corrupt Confederacy proved they could hang with the big boys. But unless Black Water royally screwed up, then...yeah....

Bye-bye, contract.

No way to change it, no way to fix it if the worst happened.

August Bragg held their future in his hands.

Chapter Seven

Seven bands. A lot of people hoping, praying to be chosen, to be one of the final three. But he'd seen everything he needed to see. By now, he understood what a successful group needed. Four of those bands displayed the qualities. While the night's audience filed out of the biggest room the Hard Rock offered, he and Micah sat to make their decision.

Which of the four top choices to eliminate?

"It hasn't been this tough before," Micah said. "Corrupt Confederacy brought it tonight."

"They did. So did Agave, Black Water, and Valkyrie Rysing." Resting his head in his hands, August took a deep breath. Should he confess?

The next forty-five minutes became a grudge match between choosing what'd be best for the label versus the music they'd enjoyed. As always, crowd participation and enthusiasm counted in the final tally.

"We're still stuck," Micah said finally.

"A bit, yes. Agave and Corrupt Confederacy both breathe much-needed life into their respective genres. Black Water has the look to go along with the sound. Valkyrie Rysing showed they can come back from flubs and still capture an audience."

"Should we let four go through?"

"No. Letting seven into tonight's round got us to this point. We need to make a firm decision. Three bands for tomorrow night." Staring at the list of pros and cons for each, he went through the mental math he always used for these types of decisions. Whom could he market? Who would pull in crowds? Who would, ultimately, make money for the label?

After racking his brain to the point of a headache, he made his decision. Clearing his throat, he forced his brain into professional mode and headed backstage to make the most mortifying introduction of his life.

***

The backstage area did *not* have enough seating. Pip ended up in the lap of Agave's front man, though she kept glancing back at Blake. *Maybe they need to get a room.* In the meantime, Joss imagined bashing Dominik's head in with any nearby blunt object. If he kept leering at her, Black Water would need a new drummer.

"They're taking a while." Rach moved the fingers of her right hand like she was following her bass frets.

"Yeah." She faced her friend, which meant leaving Dom to do his favorite thing—stare at her ass. "I need out of this room. Bad."

"Same here. Though Pipsqueak is enjoying herself."

"Seriously. Maybe she should take my date

tomorrow."

"Still hung up on that guy, huh?"

"Maybe." *Definitely.* Every time she thought about him, her entire body heated. Even now, on the most important night of her life, the phantoms of his touch traced her skin, warming her core, spreading gooseflesh along her arms, causing her nipples to harden and panties to dampen. No one meant more to her than music, but he'd gotten into her soul just the same.

"Maybe you can find him. If we get out of this room."

"Find who?"

God damn it. Blake. "None of your concern, asstwat."

He slipped his hands over her hips. She fought the urge to elbow him in the face, figuring backstage brawls wouldn't help her band's chances. "Well, you should have plenty of time to find him tomorrow, while the big boys are busy winning that contract."

"Go fuck yourself." Reaching behind her, she shoved Blake away. "Fucking hate that guy."

"I hear ya. Sexist fuckwad."

He laughed. "You're out of your league, *girls.*"

"And you're out of your intelligence bracket, uncultured swine," Joss called back.

Rachel rolled her eyes. "Remind me how you know them again?"

"My dad knows the drummer's dad. One of those."

"Gotcha."

As the minutes passed, the room grew quieter and more anxious. Pip started drumming on her knees, her soft pitter-patters creating a steady rhythm for Joss's heart to follow; Black Water reconvened in one of the corners, talking low and glancing at Joss and Rachel too often; and the others stayed quiet. How long would this take?

Finally, a knock sounded on the door. Joss's anxiety shot through the damn roof. One moment of truth, coming right up.

Micah Davis entered the room, all business in jeans and a dark gray T-shirt. Probably in his late forties, a little bit of gray at his temples, wavy hair, shrewd brown eyes, muscles for days, he reminded her of Jeffrey Dean Morgan. A little bit of salt-and-pepper stubble lined his square jaw. When he'd introduced himself the day before, Joss's attention had been focused on his words, not his appearance. But damn.

"Thanks for waiting, everyone. I'm going to make this short and sweet because I'm sure you're all tired and probably freaking out."

A weak chuckle went through the room. *Nerves. So many nerves.*

"So here we go. You guys were all fantastic, but we can only choose three for tomorrow night's show. Those three are Black Water, Agave, and Valkyrie Rysing."

Holy shit. Holy shit, holy shit, holy shit. "We did it," Joss whispered.

She met Blake's unbelieving face with the most shit-eating of shit-eating grins and coyly lifted her middle finger.

"For those I didn't call, don't be discouraged. We'll be offering feedback in the next few days and ask that you come back next year." He held open the door. "For the three I called, Mr. Bragg has a few words for you. The rest, please have a good night. You can grab your gear in the morning. Don't worry, we'll keep it safe for you."

While the others filed out, grumbling or without saying anything at all, Joss searched for a seat. *One more show, man. One more.* She practically tasted that contract.

Then August Bragg entered the room. As she stared at the face, and especially the full mouth, that had been seared into her brain from one chance encounter in a restroom, she fought the rising tide of panic.

She'd fucked the CEO of ICE Records. In a public men's room.

They were royally and completely screwed.

Chapter Eight

J ocelyn forced herself to breathe. Everything came rushing back to her—August's voice, his easy demeanor, the ice-blue eyes that grabbed her by the pussy and refused to let go, the mouth women only dreamed about kissing—and she clutched the sides of her chair to steady herself. *Deep breaths. Deep breaths. You haven't completely fucked this up. Hopefully. Maybe.*

How do I explain this to the girls?

Dressed in the same leather jacket, but this time in a silver-gray button down tucked into a pair of tight-fitting slacks, he entered the room with more poise and dignity than she could've mustered under the same circumstances. Kudos to him. In the meantime, she'd turned into a sloshy puddle of fear.

And arousal. But mostly fear.

Her entire body quaked. His eyes sparkled like blue topaz, her favorite gem, and that mouth curved into the easy smile she'd almost creamed herself over…. A shudder rocketed through her. Her nipples tightened. Fighting the ache between her thighs, she crossed her legs tight and rested her forearms on her knee. *Look away.* Suddenly, the concrete floor had the most interesting pattern of dried chewing gum she'd ever seen.

"First of all," he began, "congratulations for making it this far. You're here because you've impressed me and Micah, and because we see something in you that we can cultivate. You're obviously talented, and I am glad to hear some fresh music. ICE Records is about bringing new, unique music to the forefront."

Don't freak out. Don't puke. Don't panic.

"That being said, tomorrow night's round will give you an hour and fifteen minutes on stage. The same rules will apply—audience response, ability to carry a show, etc.—and then we will make our final decision. The winning band will sign their contract at tomorrow night's after-party."

God damn that accent. Immediately.

"We've scheduled time for each band to practice tomorrow afternoon. The show will start at 7:00 p.m., and the after-party will take place at Rendezvous at the Castillo Las Vegas following the final band's performance. Good luck to each of you. Micah and I anticipate watching you again." The way he said "watching," with a whole lot of innuendo and even more sex appeal caused Joss to look up. This time, he locked eyes with her, and her face heated. "Good night."

***

He should've told her. Should have done something more than walk into the room and make his spiel. No doubt he wouldn't have an opportunity to speak to her again, explain. Gods, he should have told her at the sound check, but her voice had captivated him. So much better live than on their beyond-impressive demo.

Damn it.

One rash decision and he'd painted himself into a corner.

I need to tell Micah. This cannot leak. If Valkyrie Rysing won the contract, every tabloid in the country would discuss this in extremely graphic detail, parsing any statement made and trying to discredit him, his company, and the band. *What a clusterfuck.*

When he pulled into the driveway of his condo, he dialed his friend, heart racing. Despite the heat, he shivered with dread, imagining his career sinking and the press hounds having a field day.

"Christ, you miss me that much already, Gus?"

"There's something I need to tell you."

"Shit. You're not dying or something, are you?"

Micah's deadpan always forced a smile. "I understand how inconvenient that'd be for you. No, I am not dying." *Yet.* "But we have an issue I'd like to contain."

All the humor went out of the other man's tone. "What happened?"

Hands shaking, August fumbled with his keys. He hesitated until he'd sat down in his favorite chair with a tumbler of scotch. "I...may have an indiscretion to confess."

A deep breath sounded into the receiver. "Tell me fast. Like ripping off a Band-Aid."

Fast. "I slept with Natalia."

The following, "Shit," was so loud August jerked the phone away from his ear. Then a flurry of expletives filled the air. After that, a crash that meant Micah had thrown his phone.

In silence, August waited out the, admittedly deserved, tirade.

"All right, I'm done. What the hell are we going to do about this?"

"No clue."

"What happened, exactly?"

August recounted the incident. "She introduced herself as Joss. I didn't know until sound checks."

"You *really* should have said something. If those girls earn their contract, and we can't take them...."

"We may lose an incredible talent because of this."

"Damn right. You. Need. To. Fix. This. Tomorrow, when they go to the Hard Rock for rehearsal, you need to *fix it*."

Easier said than done. "I'll take care of it. I assure you."

***

On stage, after the initial shock, she'd barely thought about August beyond the fact he was somewhere in the crowd. Music always gave her that kind of freedom. Even before she seriously picked up a guitar, she'd let herself go at Dejected's shows.

Ugh, best not to remember that, either.

"So you gonna tell me why you've been acting so weird?" Rachel asked.

Joss shrugged. "It's...complicated."

"Usually is with you."

Not true. Entirely. Sure, her parents divorced three days before her seventh birthday; Dad spent three hundred days a year either on the road or recording, missed birthdays, holidays, and her high school graduation; Mom drank and serial dated. Perks of being a musician's kid. Daddy's not around, so he sends presents when he remembers. Not unheard of by any means. But it made her run and hide from the truth too often.

"You really wanna hear this?"

"Of course."

"That guy I fucked? August. Fucking. Bragg."

Rachel's face crumbled as dramatically as a building that'd been blown up with dynamite. She kept quiet until they were in the hotel room. Pip went to grab a shower, leaving Joss at her friend's mercy. "Please tell me this is the worst possible April Fool's Day prank in the universe."

"Last I checked, it ain't April."

"Do you have *any* idea what this'll do to us?"

"Trust me, I've done nothing *but* contemplate every possible scenario. None of this is sitting right with me."

"We should withdraw. Pack up and go home." Shaking her head, Rachel started to pace, tapping her fingertips against her leg like it was her bass, working out the frenetic energy Joss's confession caused, no doubt about to split at the seams.

"I'm sorry, Rach." The pleading sound in her voice grated on her; almost like when she tried to placate Anderson before he ditched her.

"It doesn't matter," she said softly. "If ICE signs us, we won't be able to tell if it's because of *us* or because of *you*."

Joss sank into the nearest chair. "I fucked our chances—literally—before we ever got on stage."

"Well, hey, we don't know we're getting signed. Black Water's sounding pretty damn good."

"Yeah, but they're assholes, so there's that at least."

After a few minutes of silence, her friend said, "Not like this'll be our only chance, right?"

Joss didn't have it in her to respond.

Chapter Nine

Only Valkyrie Rysing arrived on time for their rehearsal. In fact, they were early, regardless of it being 11:00 a.m. After the announcement last night, August figured they'd run late; perhaps they'd gone out for celebratory drinks. Part of him hoped for it, wished for more time to procrastinate.

But no. They showed up. Early. What sort of musician shows up early?

The kind who wants to win.

They patiently waited for Agave to clear off their gear before setting up. Joss focused on the tasks in front of her, setting up her pedal board just so and fiddling with the height of the mic stand. Though she'd tried to appear casual in the same washed-out Led Zeppelin T-shirt and the black jeans she'd been wearing when they met, her set jaw and hard eyes displayed her determination for all to see. Pippa and Rachel matched her, and the stage threatened to combust with their combined fire.

He wanted them to win.

Bias be damned, he wanted them to get the

contract. Not because of Joss, or what they'd done together, but because he saw passion in the three of them. A passion he shared. A passion that once forced him to choose his dreams and ambitions over his family.

Over the years, he'd regretted his decision. Sometimes he contemplated giving up. That day, watching three amazing musicians dominate a stage without an audience, his heart told him he'd made the right choice. On both accounts.

Now to repair the damage he'd done. Maybe there was still a way to give Valkyrie Rysing their contract. If they earned it.

A night of tossing and turning made for a shitty morning. Joss rubbed her eyes to appease the headache starting at her temples, but the damn stubborn thing refused to abate. Rehearsal wouldn't help, either, but they needed to get their new song down. The rest of their show, she could do in her sleep at this point. But the new song had to be enough to top Black Water. Blake's bullshit made this personal.

No matter what happened—with August, with Black Water, with any of it—she planned to walk away with her head held high.

It'd be better with a record deal.

By the way her skin heated, she figured August was there, probably somewhere unobtrusive, gauging their rehearsal. The thought made her stomach churn, but not how she'd expected. Rather than relive the previous night's dread, she let the knowledge invigorate her. She'd make sure he'd regret choosing someone else.

With the initial re-setup out of the way, they played through "Soulless" to get the sound and staging right. The night before, they'd gotten a pretty generic light show, like everyone else. This time around, she intended to have the full effect.

"You sure you want to do the new song?" Rachel asked.

"Oh, yeah. I'm not leaving Vegas without performing it." She strummed the opening chords. "But it still needs some work." *A lot of work.*

"Will we have enough time?"

No. "We have to." This one would be their trump card. The song of her heart. *Nobody can top it.*

August waited until the music stopped. Then, he counted to three and stepped out of his hiding spot. When Joss saw him, she froze, and her beautiful green eyes went wide.

"Hi," she said.

"Hello." He forced a smile. "May I speak to you for a moment?"

With a curt nod, she followed him away from the stage. Everything he'd hoped to say stuck in his throat. Thankfully, she started. "This is a huge clusterfuck, isn't it?"

"It is. Micah had no idea before he made the announcement. Truly, I wish I'd never told him anything."

She blinked a couple of times. "You didn't tell him. Till after."

"Correct."

"But you pick."

"I gave him my input, but I ultimately left the decision to Micah." He lifted her chin to ensure she met his gaze, ashamed at the dread radiating from her. "You and your band are talented, Joss. Valkyrie Rysing cemented its place before we ever met."

"Okay. Okay...." Immediately, her breathing slowed, and the fear left her face.

"You and your band are here on your own merit. What happened between us was...." *Amazing, fantastic.*

"Hot as fuck," she said with a little smile.

"Agreed." The urge to kiss her nearly overwhelmed him. But it was imperative he retained his decorum, regardless of his body's carnal intentions.

"This is for the best, right?"

"It is." As much as he hated it. "I believe you and your bandmates have a contract to win, Miss Bishop."

Hell yeah, they did. She returned to Pip and Rachel with a smile on her face and a fire in her belly that had mostly nothing to do with August. The girls stared at her with expectation, and she took a deep breath. "We're going to kick ass and take names tonight, ladies."

"You sure about the song, Joss?" Pip asked.

"Positive. We got this. Besides, we gotta show Black Water that women can kick ass better'n the big boys."

"Hell yeah, we do." Rachel clapped Joss on the shoulder. "No matter what happens, we're gonna rock the shit out of Vegas and leave this city with our heads held high."

That sounded so perfect. So right. She just hoped she didn't fuck this up.

Chapter Ten

As the last strains of Agave's final song faded and the crowd roared with applause and screams, Jocelyn checked her reflection one more time. She demanded perfection tonight, from her spiked hair to her spiked boots. No mistakes. *No pressure.*

Before leaving the rehearsal, she'd gone over the effects she and her bandmates wanted for the show—lights, sounds, anything and everything—and then she holed up in the hotel room to think way too much about shit that may or may not matter anymore. Anderson, Ty, the future, the past. Putting it all behind her for one night proved difficult but necessary. Time to focus on the most important show of her life.

And now she stood in the back room, alone, staring into the mirror and not seeing anything. The thoughts from earlier that afternoon tumbled around in her head again, drawing her away from her mental checklist. She took a few deep breaths. A knock at the door caused her to jump, and she nearly twisted an ankle in the stiletto boots she insisted on wearing.

The door opened slowly, like in one of those stupid horror movies Anderson loved so damn much. August stuck his head in, and, finding her alone, the rest of him followed suit.

"I didn't mean to interrupt," he said. "I simply wanted to wish you luck."

Heart in her throat, she smiled. "Thank you."

He stepped closer, one hand fisted at his side, and the other nervously tapping against his jean-clad thigh. "I...I'm not supposed to speak to the bands until the after-party, but I wanted to give you something."

"August, you don't—"

"I know," he said, stepping a little closer, "but I need to." Unclenching his hand, he revealed a gold necklace with a harp charm. "In Norse mythology, Bragi is the god of poetry and music. The legend goes that Odin first received the gift of poetry, but he used it rarely, so he gave it to his son, Bragi. Upon the young god's birth, dwarves gifted him a magic harp made of gold." A wistful smile graced his perfect lips. "It is said he charmed everyone with his music, from the gods of the heavens to Hel, the goddess of the underworld." Then he glanced up at her through long, dark lashes. "I've kept this charm for quite a while, a trinket my grandmother picked up because she liked the scrollwork on the harp's frame. I never enjoyed performing, but I kept it anyway." He moved behind her and draped the necklace around her neck. After he clasped it, he continued. "Now, though, I have met someone I feel encompasses Bragi's spirit. Someone who can charm any audience, any person."

"Even you?" she asked, for some reason uncertain.

"More than anyone else." With a halfhearted smile, he left.

***

Electricity zipped through the air, almost enough to drive August from her mind. She fingered the harp charm and ran her fingertip over the runes etched into the frame. One more show to determine her future. One more night to determine the rest of her life.

The 1Night Stand date crept into her thoughts again. More and more, she wanted to meet this mysterious person Madame Eve found for her, in the hope he'd be able to help her forget the one man who'd made her feel good enough.

With their gear set up, Joss let the first strains of her warmup filter through the Marshall stacks on either side of the stage. She adored the way her Fernandes Ravelle Elite sounded like pure rock, and, combined with the stacks, she fell deeper in love with her pawn shop find. Someone missed the hell out of a killer guitar. Their loss, her gain.

As Rachel joined in, Joss detected a different sound, one that complemented the Elite perfectly. Then Pip started her gentle rolls on the snare, followed by a soothing pattern on the toms. The warmup resembled a lullaby that lulled the audience into a false sense of calm, and the six-eight time signature let Joss and Rachel stretch their fingers without strain. Jocelyn found her happy place.

When the warmup ended and the stage lights snapped on, the crowd lost their fucking minds, to the point their roars drowned out the monitors. She glanced to Rachel and grinned at the sight of her Thunderbird slung low across her hips. Appropriate that the TB's first show be the game changer.

August caught her attention with lust in his ice-blue eyes that sent white-hot desire through her body. *Oh, yeah. Time to rock some faces off.*

Without an introduction, they lit into "Rise," and Joss nailed it. No flubs, no mistakes, no being caught off guard.

The show couldn't have gone more perfectly. The crowd ate them up, and watching Blake sulk by the bar made her night all the better. Plus, Pipsqueak got to show off her crazy drum prowess to a *lot* of hootin' and hollerin'. Glad they finally got to experience what she and Rachel heard every time they rehearsed.

"All right, guys, we got one more for y'all." At the chorus of boos, she shook her head. "I know, I know. I mean, *I* could go all night, but it ain't my call."

Rach's haunting bass line floated through the air, mournful and lonesome. The crowd stilled, and a hush fell over the room.

"This last song is a special one," Joss said. "I wrote it a few years back, about a boy, like most everything else is. But then I realized something." She strummed the opening chord. "It wasn't about him. It was about me. This is 'Broken Folklore.'"

The song started in a whisper, with her dueting with Rachel's bass.

I reminisce the things you've told me
Glimpsing lies your life's become
I surmise what you've abandoned
Then I mourn what's come undone

Through the second half of the verse, she built to a crescendo.

There exists more than you've shown me
Living life deaf, blind, and dumb
In a world of swords and dragons
The fairest fantasy is homespun

Then, back to the softness for the chorus.

Lies look so fair wrapped in metaphor
So much to hide in certain vagueness
But pretty words and broken folklore
Can't seduce a mind unshaken
Enchanting words won't hypnotize
A string of lies can't change the fact
If you'd reopen just one blind eye
You'd see that there is no. Way. Back.

She screamed the last three words, and Pip's cymbal-crash brought the crowd to life. Heavy guitar riffs reminiscent of Metallica's filled the room. Screams and cheering almost drowned out her monitor. Exactly the reaction she'd hoped for.

Gaze at the sun too long, child brightness
Taint your vision for all time
Hold your breath and wade in deeper
To your delusion of falsely fine
In your realm of satisfaction
Guard the ridges of your mind
Censor, sort— make your world sweeter
Sate your guilt, but leave the landmine

As she went through the chorus again, she sought out August, and her heartbeat double-timed at the heat radiating from him. Time to seal the deal with an epic guitar solo.

Her fingers flew across the frets with minds of their own. Closing her eyes, she let the music carry her, lift her up, and guide her. Regardless of how the competition turned out, she always had that feeling to depend on.

The drums and bass dropped out, leaving her doing her best Kirk Hammett impression with a nutjob solo that most guitarists wouldn't even try, especially on a song they'd never performed.

Of course, she wasn't most guitarists.

The solo led into the bridge, and the audience rioted. Softening, harkening back to the first verse, she sang the last barely above a whisper.

Calm your conscience with poetic lies
Speak what may appease my ears
Repress your shame and say again
"You mean so much" to dry my tears
Guide me through the storyline
Let me rehearse my part, my dear
Line and scenes, approach the end
Where the finale's forever veered

In her mind, she counted the beats. *One, two, three, four.*

Lies look so fair wrapped in metaphor
So much to hide in certain vagueness
But pretty words and broken folklore
Can't seduce a mind unshaken

Enchanting words won't hypnotize
A string of lies can't change the fact
If you'd reopen just one blind eye
You'd see that there is No. Way. Back

The song ended on her scream. A few moments of silence passed, followed by the eruption of a frenzied crowd.

They'd done it. They'd fucking done it.

Micah's enthusiasm bruised and overwhelmed him. Rubbing his arm, August prepared for another onslaught. Sure enough, the older man's open palm connected with his bicep, and he repeatedly mouthed, "Holy shit!" and various other combinations of expletives. Though more subdued, August shared his enthusiasm. Valkyrie Rysing brought the performance of their lives.

Once the music died and the crowd settled down a bit, Micah said, "There's no way Black Water can beat them. No fucking way."

From the dejected fall of his face and the slump of his shoulders, Blake Young realized it, too.

Still, the final band required its time in the spotlight. As far as he was concerned, though, the ladies had won the night.

And Joss had stolen his heart.

A shame he couldn't give it to her. If he maintained any hope of signing Valkyrie Rysing, he, August Bragg, the man, must relinquish the desire, the lust, the respect to August Bragg, the CEO. He'd meet his 1Night Stand and pray she'd be enough to help him forget his Natalia. His Joss.

In the meantime, he'd listen to Black Water and contemplate his speech for the after-party

Chapter Eleven

Squirreled away in the back room, Joss sat with her bandmates, celebratory brew in hand. "To the future, bitches."

"Hell yes." Rachel clinked her bottle with theirs and smiled that devil smile. "And to Black Water for having to suck it."

"Did you see the look on Blake's face? You'da thought we'd pissed all over his favorite guitar."

"Or his favorite hooker," Pip muttered.

Joss burst into the giggles that only come from alcohol. "You know that's right. Ain't no woman gonna go anywhere near that unless she's gettin' paid real good."

"Your accent is so much stronger when you're excited," Rachel teased.

"Then you'd best get used to hearin' it, darlin'," she said in an exaggerated twang. "'Cause I am one excited bitch."

"And *we'd* best get back to the hotel. We have an after-party to get ready for. And you have a date to get ready for."

Groaning, Joss set her empty beer bottle on the

table. "Thanks for killing my buzz."

"Why does it have to be a buzzkill? Why can't you have a good time with someone? It's one night."

"Yeah. 'It's one night.' That's what I said to Ty the first time I begged him to come over. That's what I told Anderson when we first hooked up. I'm not sure I have another 'one night' in me."

"What are you afraid of?" Pip asked quietly.

Heaving a deep breath, she said, "Of wanting someone so bad I lose myself again. Trust me, Ty wasn't the only one consumed. I just burned to ash faster." Suddenly full of nervous energy, she stood and started pacing. "I won't do it again. I can't."

"You can."

She stopped pacing and faced Rachel. "No. I'm concentrating on the band. We won that fucking contract. You and I both know it. If I get involved with someone, what happens then? What happens to us?"

"We'll figure it out. We figured it out after Ty and Anderson, and we'll keep figuring it out until we get it right." Rising from her chair, Rachel placed a comforting hand on Joss's arm. Warmth flooded Jocelyn's system and calmed her to a point where fear no longer blinded her, though, inside, she still shook like an animal caught in a trap.

"One night, right?" she asked.

"One night."

"And then?"

Rachel smiled. "We'll figure it out."

***

The ladies' performance obviously shook Blake

Young. He missed cues, fumbled and slurred through lyrics, and butchered notes any beginning guitar player managed without issue. "How many drinks you reckon he's had?" Micah asked.

August shook his head. "Enough to make our decision for us."

After Valkyrie Rysing's amazing show, Black Water's lead singer wrote off his band and made good friends with the bartender, a buxom blonde who'd been more than happy to help him drown his sorrows. Blake staggered to the stage, tripped once or twice over his own feet, and…. Both August and Micah winced at the unintentional feedback from the speakers.

Pathetic. "My decision is made. I will see you at the after-party."

The other man gave him a thumbs-up. "Don't waste your eardrums on this one. I'm gonna hang around, see if we have a Blues Brothers' situation."

"I doubt 'Rawhide' will save them."

Taking one last look at the stage, he turned on his heel. *Time to draw up the paperwork.*

And figure out how to tell Joss good-bye.

***

In his home office, August typed up the contract on autopilot. The future taunted him, at times showing him success and, at others, leading him to conclude his father had been right all along. Though ICE Records' bands dominated rock music, failure loomed on the periphery. Business came with risks. Music flowed and ebbed like ocean tides. Still, he determined to stay afloat, regardless of how he currently drowned.

He pushed Joss from his mind long enough to shower and redress for the after-party-slash-date. Staring at the mirror, he automatically adjusted his ice-blue tie and pinned the ICE logo-embossed tie clip to it. *Joss.* Slicked back his hair. *You can't.* Tugged on his silver blazer. *Have her.*

Swallowing his fear and his pride, he reviewed the contract once more and prayed Micah understood his decision. The company's future came first. He'd made certain of it for four years.

Meeting someone else while still infatuated with the gorgeous redhead seemed less than fair, to him or his date. Still, pursuing Joss created a conflict of interest if he meant to sign the band, and the dreams of those three women weighed heavier on his heart than his misguided desire.

Checking the knot of his tie one more time, he mentally rehearsed his speech. The night needed to be flawless. Press from major music magazines, local radio stations, and gods knew who else would be attending. Last year's winner, a progressive rock band that had stayed number one on Billboard's charts for fifty-four straight weeks, would play a set to showcase ICE Records' brand of talent, and then....

Then he would be her boss. Once the ink dried on the contract, he'd disappear back into the shadows of the corporation.

Chapter Twelve

Jocelyn held up the scrap of emerald-green fabric Rachel claimed to be a dress and cocked an eyebrow.

"In the email, I mentioned you'd be wearing a green cocktail dress, okay?" Rach huffed. "This is not a jeans-and-leather-jacket occasion."

"Yeah, I read the testimonials on that damn website." Translation—she'd spent hours scouring 1Night Stand's site and reading everything she found. From what she saw, the claims were true. People who went through them found twue wuv. Happily ever afters. Soul mates. All the shit she no longer believed in, if she ever had. "You honestly believe I'm gonna meet Mr. Jocelyn Richards tonight?"

"Gonna make him take your name, huh?"

Glaring, she tossed the dress back on the bed. "I'm not doing this. Send Pippa if you want to send anyone at all."

At the sound of her name, Pip turned around. "I'm good, thanks."

"Remember," Rachel said, "it's one night. If Hell freezes and you end up not liking the guy, then you can chew my ass over it all the way back to L.A."

"Fine. I'll put it on after the announcement." Why fight anymore? She'd given in to fear for too long. Time to see if those testimonials were true.

***

Micah Davis met them outside of Rendezvous, dressed to the nines in an ice-blue suit that accentuated his muscular frame and the silver flecks in his hair, making him look distinguished and sexy as hell. Joss shivered as thoughts of the last time she stood outside the club rushed through her like class-five rapids.

"Evening, ladies," he said. "Right this way."

He led them through a massive crowd of bodies writhing and swaying to Broken Halo, a band whose debut album she'd listened to on repeat for three straight weeks until Rachel hid the CD. The club itself was gorgeous, mixing classic Greek-style columns and ceiling frescos with more modern colors and décor. An odd combination of styles that only worked in Vegas.

At a door marked *VIP ONLY*, Micah knocked a few times. A man so muscular he had no neck answered and motioned them in. With a wink, the veep left them.

"Sweet baby Jesus on a pancake, look at all this." Spinning in a slow circle, Rachel took in the sights while Joss headed for a vacant seat. What sort of sadist planned a life-altering date on a life-changing night? She took the champagne a waitress offered and settled back against the plush cushions of the most comfortable chair she'd ever sat in. The VIP room proved even more impressive than the club, with low lights that cast a serene dark-blue glow over the black walls and crisp-white marble tile. Broken Halo's music came through as a bass beat thudding against the wall. Last year, they'd sat in this same room, waiting for the announcement that would change everything. Joss hoped they'd share the same fate.

Glancing around, she took note of the different pieces of art adorning the space with *Rolling Stone* covers and a few band posters covering the walls, until she spotted, on one of the shelves, a statue of a man with a long beard playing a golden harp. *Bragi.*

Her fingertips brushed over the symbols on the charm around her neck. She hadn't had the heart to take off the necklace, and if her date asked her about it, she'd tell him the truth. Once she figured out what the truth really was.

The door opened again, and Agave entered, followed by Black Water, minus Blake and Dominick. Rachel tensed and sat next to her while Pip struck up a conversation with Agave's front man.

"Looks like they're getting cozy," Joss said.

"Yeah." Rachel swallowed. "Wonder where Blake is."

"No idea." Wherever he was, it couldn't be good.

***

What the hell is this ruckus? August checked his watch. Broken Halo still had another half hour in their set, but no music met him at the entrance to Rendezvous. Rather, a fight welcomed him to the club. A fight between Blake Young and Eric

Hawthorne, Broken Halo's bass player. Adjusting his tie, August strode toward the stage. In his peripheral vision, he spotted Micah doing the same while using the communicator on his wrist to contact security.

August reached the stage first and muscled between the two. Eric stepped back, but the other man decided to take a blind swing, which August blocked with ease. With no fucks left for the other man's antics, he landed a precise fist to Blake's jaw, unsatisfied by the crunch of bone. Security arrived moments later, but too late to save the singer from a broken jaw.

"I want him out. Bar him from the club and give him to the police." Spoiled children of wealthy parents rarely went through life without consequence. Let Blake have his sooner rather than later.

After the band gave security their statements, they resumed playing. Micah dragged him toward the back of the club. "Hell of a southpaw you got there. I'm surprised Young got back up after that."

"Hardheaded men tend to rebound better from physical violence." Shaking his head, he took a glass of champagne from a passing waitress.

"Should probably ice those knuckles, man."

"There will be time for that. How are our other bands holding up?"

"Far as I can tell, they're fine. Got to tell you, though, our Valkyries are dressed to kill."

August snickered. *Our Valkyries.* "I expect no less from them."

After that, they settled into companionable silence while the band finished its set. Going over his speech one more time, he gripped the manila folder, knowing it held the future in more ways than one, and prayed he'd made the right decision for both his head and his heart. The last song finished, and uproarious applause filled his ears. He lived for these moments, what he dreamed of. Pure joy from music, love in its simplest form. Like a ghost, he glided through the crowd, and no one noticed him until he took the stage.

He nodded to Micah, who went to retrieve the bands from the back. He couldn't look at Joss, not right now. To avoid it, he focused on the envelope in his hand. "I hope everyone has enjoyed the weekend," he started.

The crowd roared to life once again.

"As many of you know, every June ICE Records likes to take over Las Vegas for a weekend to showcase new talent. What some of you may not know is that we utilize this weekend to sign said new talent. Last year's winners, Broken Halo, have been entertaining you—in more ways than one, apparently—and this year's winners are waiting in the wings for their opportunity."

More clapping and screaming filled the room.

"We began this weekend with an unheard-of seven bands, when we typically stay with six. However, there is quite a bit of talent in the world, and a...what is the term Micah likes to use...a metric shit-ton in this room. Three bands rose above the rest. Two of them, Agave and Valkyrie Rysing are here tonight. Black Water disqualified themselves when their lead singer tried to punch his potential boss." More laughter. "Agave's sound is something I've been searching for, for quite a while. They bring a solid stage show, a commanding performance, and a technical prowess missing from bands these days." He took a breath. "Valkyrie Rysing is pure passion, a pinch of volatility, and a talent that will haunt your sleep." With shaking hands, he opened the envelope. "ICE Records is pleased to present a contract tonight. To Agave."

The crowd erupted, and in the back of the room, Agave's members high-fived and clapped and hugged. Next to them, the ladies of Valkyrie Rysing held hands, heads bowed with disappointment.

"I'm not finished," he said with a broad grin. "In a weekend of anomalies, we are offering another. Valkyrie Rysing, I have a present for you as well."

Though he didn't want to, he met Joss's disbelieving face. His goddess's mouth hung slightly open, and the lights caught on glistening tears.

"For the first time in the five years we have put on this contest, my brain failed to make a decision. So, I am following my heart. Congratulations to our winners—Agave *and* Valkyrie Rysing!"

It couldn't be true. No way in hell that just happened. But Pip's yell of, "Suck it, Blake!" and Rachel's bear hug confirmed it.

"We won?"

"We fucking won," Rach said. "We did it, Joss!"

In a daze, she followed her bandmates toward the table where Micah Davis stood with the contracts in hand. Contracts. Two of them. *One for Agave and one for...us.*

The after-party kicked into full swing behind them, but Joss's attention remained on the piece of paper in front of her, with Pippa's and Rachel's signatures in dark-blue ink.

And after this, a date? How?

"Congratulations, ladies." Micah took the pen from Joss's fingers and scrawled an elegant signature. "Welcome to ICE Records."

Chapter Thirteen

Drinks. Hors d'oeuvres. More drinks. Music. Dancing. Pip and Rachel appeared to be having a great time, but Joss's mind still reeled, and that question niggled the back of her mind like a chigger she couldn't find: Was it because of their talent, or because August had a thing for her?

And she, admittedly, had one for him?

Over and over, she told herself it didn't matter. People would stand up and take notice when they went on tour—*ohmigod tour*—and they'd hear it on the albums. If the world demanded she spend the rest of her days proving she'd earned this, then she'd do it, and she'd kick ass the whole way.

Feeling invincible for the first time ever, she slipped away from the party and found the "dress." One-shouldered, with an asymmetrical hem that barely covered her business and cutouts in the back...she felt more porn star than rock star, but her date expected the emerald color.

Madame Eve, you'd better be as good as they say.

When she stepped back into the room, she

searched for an open spot that'd allow her date to see her—as if he'd miss her in this getup—but nothing suited her. She settled on a wall toward the back lined with some comfy-looking couches and found a seat to people watch. A waitress brought her champagne, and though the last thing she needed was more alcohol, she sipped the bubbly and let it calm her last few nerves while the rest recovered from the evening's shock.

Lost in her thoughts and the crowd, she didn't hear anyone come up, but a man cleared his throat. And when she saw him, she almost spilled her drink. "August."

"Is this seat taken?"

"Um, well, I'm waiting for a...date, actually." *Christ, Joss, pull it together, woman.*

"1Night Stand?" he asked.

"How did you...?"

He sighed and handed her the printout of an email.

August,
I have found for you an exquisite match, a woman who embodies all you love in music and life. She is spirited, caring, and passionate, but she has been mistreated by both herself and others. Handle her with care, and she will be a perfect companion for you.

Your future awaits you dressed in emeralds and crowned with fire.
Sincerely yours,
Madame Eve

"Holy shit." The world stopped. Joss wasn't sure

if she breathed or if her heart kept beating. All she knew was this email and the man who'd given it to her. The man she wanted to trust with her body if not her heart. "What do I say to that?"

"That you'll try? That you'll let me try? That...." She finally met his eyes, saw in his face the earnestness she'd craved and feared for so long. "That you'll give me one night with you?"

"What about the contract? Won't it look bad if we leave together?" From her relationship with Anderson, she remembered painfully well how tabloids manipulated photos, and she'd noticed a few photogs milling around. This spelled disaster for a career taking its first steps.

"Micah is capable of handling any negative press, but I understand your worry." He stood. "We needn't go through with this, Jocelyn. Forgive me."

"August, wait."

To her surprise, he did. Taking his hand, so warm and perfect in hers, she coaxed him back onto the sofa. "I...I need this. Need you."

"You're certain?"

"As long as you can handle getting Jocelyn Richards and not Natalia Bishop."

"Jocelyn Richards is all I want."

They left the party with ease. Few people glanced their way, and, with Joss's wardrobe change, he thought fewer made any sort of connection. He led her to the parking lot, and, in the cool night air, he thought he could finally breathe.

"Where are we going?"

"I have a home not far from here if you're

comfortable going there. If not—"

"No, that sounds awesome. I really need a break from the hotel."

Opening the car door for her, he ensured her comfort before moving to the driver's side. She stretched her long legs and leaned back. "This," she said, gesturing to the cocktail dress, "not my idea, by the way."

"Whose was it? I would like to thank them." Though he doubted he'd voice his exact thought, considering how she squirmed and tugged at the skirt's fabric, tamping down his arousal at seeing more of her body proved difficult. He ached to touch her, to devote more time to worshipping his beautiful goddess, if only for the night.

"Rachel's," she said with a throaty laugh. "I almost refused."

"I'm glad you listened to her."

Her hand covered his on the gearshift. "Me, too. Can I be honest with you?"

"I certainly encourage it."

"I'm kinda freaking out. I mean, this weekend changed my life. I went from being this insecure bitch with daddy issues to being an insecure bitch with daddy issues with a music contract. And now this beautiful, perfect man is taking me to his house." She paused. "You're not going to kill me, right?"

"The only violence tonight was against Blake Young, and I didn't intend it." Sparing a glance at her, he said, "You're safe."

The smile she gave him in response almost brought him to orgasm right there. "That's all I've ever wanted to hear."

Along the drive, they talked about their pasts,

about how August left Iceland to pursue his dream, how Jocelyn's father almost ruined hers. "I'm also freakishly codependent," she admitted. "I apologize in advance."

"We'll discuss boundaries, if necessary. You're stronger than you realize, and, I assure you, I am not going anywhere unless you tell me to go."

"You say that now...."

"And I will continue to say it until you believe me, and then I will say it more to ensure you still believe me." As he pulled into the driveway, he sensed her trepidation. "Are you certain? I'll take you back to the hotel."

"No. I want you. I want whatever this thing is between us." She leaned in and brushed her lips against his. "Take me inside and make love to me."

"Gladly."

Threading his fingers through her hair, he pulled her close and kissed her with far more patience and control than he thought he possessed. Everything Madame Eve said proved true, and he intended to show Jocelyn she deserved better than life had given her, starting tonight. She yielded to his touch, opened her mouth to allow him access, and he took full advantage, exploring her with his tongue. His other hand rested on her shoulder; she took it and moved it down to cup her breast. Instantly, her nipple pebbled, and she moaned like a cat purring, the vibration going straight to his straining erection. "We should get inside before the neighbors get a show they don't want."

"It's dark enough, don't you think? They shouldn't be able to see us unless they *really* look." The vixen slid her dress strap down her arm and revealed her perfect breasts. "I'd sure as hell want to get a good look at you."

Reaching between his legs, he eased his seat back and motioned for her to come to him. Eager, she straddled him. He alternated between licking and suckling her nipple while her breathy moans and sighs filled the tight space. Like a furnace, her heat radiated through the thin fabric of her panties and his trousers. No way to get to her like this, to bury himself in the scent and the taste of her like he wanted. If she gave him tonight, fully, he'd live the rest of his life knowing he'd found perfection, but he wouldn't let her go before dawn.

"God, August," she panted. "You're so fucking hard. I still remember how good you felt inside me."

"As do I." Slipping his hand between their bodies, he hiked up her dress. "I need to taste you, Joselyn." Before she replied he slid her panties aside and exposed her hot, wet sex. Gods, she was soaked already. With his fingers, he opened her folds and found her tight bundle of nerves begging to be stroked, licked, kissed, sucked. "I want to take you inside and pleasure you however you desire."

"Right now, I kind of desire to fuck you in the car."

Or that.

"Let the seat down a little."

He complied. With the new position, she leaned over him, hands planted on either side of the headrest. In the light from a nearby streetlamp, her eyes glowed like emeralds, and the sweet scent of her arousal met his nose.

Working his belt and pants loose with one hand, he fished for his wallet with the other. Joss grabbed it from him and found the condom. "Planning to get lucky, huh?"

"One should always be prepared for unforeseen circumstances."

"Smart man." With her other hand she helped him free his cock from the confinement of his pants. He nearly sighed with relief. "I swear to God, August, you've got to have the biggest cock I've about ever seen. I don't know what I want more, that monster in my pussy or my mouth."

"We have plenty of time, Joss."

"Hell yeah, we do. You want to pleasure me, right?"

"Right."

After she rolled on the condom, she eased herself onto his member, groaning as her muscles stretched to let him in, and positioned herself to ride him. Being inside her again was pure magic, and this time, he knew her name, knew *her*. A connection formed.

Resting his hands on her hips, he allowed her to move at whatever tempo she desired. If she wanted to speak—and part of him hoped she would—he wanted her to say whatever she pleased.

"Goddamn," she moaned. "You wanna know what really makes me hot, August?"

"Fucking in a car?"

"That's definitely on the list." She came down hard and eased herself back off, alternating strokes and clouding his vision with lust. "Something I've ever tried once, but I got off so hard I forgot how to play guitar the next day?"

"Tell me."

Still undulating her hips in that torturous rhythm, she lowered her lips to the shell of his ear.

Her hot, panting breaths added to the torment of his beautiful Valkyrie. "I want you to tie me up and do anything to me that you've ever wanted to do to a woman."

"As long as you still remember how to play guitar, I'll do whatever you ask."

She laughed again. "Don't worry. I got that part covered this time."

Then she raised up, her back pressed against the steering wheel, and using his shoulders for support she fucked him. There was no other thought, no other word. Like their time before, animalistic need poured into them both. But he needed so much more of her. Gripping her tight, he slammed her down on his cock hard enough for her tits to bounce. Unable to resist, he pulled a nipple into his mouth and sucked, grazing her with teeth and soothing with tongue, until she cried out. Gods, she felt so damned good he wanted to keep going forever, but his body betrayed him, his balls tightened, and he spilled his seed into her as her muscles gripped him and milked him for everything he offered.

Seconds passed then minutes, with neither of them speaking. His hunger for her temporarily sated, he lifted her off his lap and helped her settle into the passenger side. "I have never had sex in a car," he said.

"You need to get out more, August."

Once he got her inside his house—scratch that, *mansion*—she understood exactly why he never left. The place was immaculate, all marble floors and expensive *everything*. "You practically live in an art museum."

"I like fine things. They were never valued in my family."

"Like music?"

"Especially music." Taking her hand, he led her down the hallway, which opened up to a living space bigger than her current apartment on the right, and a huge kitchen on the left. Farther down, he stopped at a closed door. "Let me show you something."

He opened the door and flicked on a light. Joss's heart nearly stopped at the sight of the instruments contained inside, which included a cabinet specifically for the three unbelievable violins housed within. "Temperature and moisture controlled," he said. "I have a separate cabinet for acoustics on the other side."

"This is literally Heaven. I died and you're the smoking-hot angel who takes me to Heaven, and this is it." She was babbling, but so what? In front of her, to the left and right of her, and above her, was displayed everything she'd ever wanted. But the showpiece? The harp in the center of the room. She knew nothing about harps, but from the craftsmanship of the body, this one cost an arm and a leg. "Tell me you play this."

"Shall I seduce you with the music of my people?"

"Only appropriate since I seduced you with the music of *my* people."

With a grin, he rolled up his sleeves and sat on the stool positioned behind the instrument. In the next few breaths, a soft, sweet melody filled the room. Joss held her breath while August's fingers deftly moved over the strings, and as the music swelled, his hands moved faster until they were nearly a blur. She'd never heard this song; hell, she hadn't heard music like this at all, and once it died, the emotion bled out of her like water bursting through a dam until all that remained were her racing heart and the need to mount her date where he sat.

"What did you just play?" she asked.

"It's an old song, one I learned in my youth. My grandmother owned a harp and insisted I learn. So I did. I competed," he added with a nonchalant shrug.

"You mean you won."

"I did. Does that impress you?"

"So far, there's nothing about you that doesn't impress me."

He smiled, somewhat melancholy, and stood, offering his hand. Heart hammering, she took it, falling for him more and more with each passing breath.

Her boss.

God damn it.

Chapter Fourteen

The rest of August's house tour became an indescribable torture of history lessons and foreplay. Gape at a painting, learn everything about the artist with a hand on your breast and the other stroking your inner thigh. Make a comment about a statue, get a breathy explanation of the myth depicted plus a couple of well-placed nips on your neck and ears. By the time they reached the bedroom, she was full-on ready to burst.

In her mind, it'd already happened no fewer than fifty-five times. August taking her into the bedroom, ripping off her dress, throwing her to the bed, and having his way with her. Fireworks, explosions, a marching band, the whole works. Probably the alcohol talking, but still, a girl had to dream.

When he opened the door, revealing a bedroom decked out in the same ice-blue, silver, and gray as ICE Records' logo, she stifled a gasp. Minimalist, understated, beautiful. The walls were covered in silver wallpaper with a slight sheen to it. Gauzy gray curtains flanked the floor-to-ceiling windows. Here and there, he'd hung beautiful paintings she wanted to soak in, but the way he stroked her body made it impossible to focus. He slid the shoulder of her dress down, lingering touches igniting a deeper need within her. His scent filled her brain, and she relaxed into him, winding one arm around his neck while her other hand stroked his outer thigh through the softest denim she'd ever touched.

Could this night be any more perfect?

August pulled the dress completely off and explored her exposed skin. Kisses covered the back of her neck, her shoulders, and down farther as he bent her forward. Fingertips traced down her spine and she shivered, gooseflesh rising on her arms and thighs and nipples pebbling. Her legs turned to jelly. Moaning softly, she braced against the side of his bed and craned her neck to see him. Kneeling behind her, he continued his perusal of her body, hands and mouth and tongue exploring parts of her left untouched—inner thighs, the backs of her legs, even behind her knees. Without missing a beat, he slipped her panties down and palmed her hot sex, thumb stroking her throbbing clit while his fore and middle fingers worked inside her in a lazy rhythm meant to arouse, not satisfy. She started to step out of her high heels. "Leave them on," came August's gentle command.

He stood. She sensed his heat before she felt his erection in the cleft of her ass. She imagined him naked, picturesque, and beautiful like the statue of Bragi she'd seen. Reaching behind her, she yelped when her wrists were snagged and pinned above her head. "You enjoy being restrained?"

Heart hammering like a double bass, she nodded.

"Stay exactly as you are."

She swallowed. Letting her ex tie her up was one thing—literally, one thing that had happened once and, no matter how she hinted, never happened again—but allowing someone she'd known for a few days at most? On the outside it looked like the worst idea ever. But she knew she could trust him. For the first time in a while, she agreed with what her heart was telling her brain. She was safe.

Standing bone-still, she counted her breaths until he came back. She didn't look up, didn't try to cheat and peek from beneath her eyelashes. Silk brushed against her skin, starting from between her shoulder blades and feathering down to her ass. What would he do to her once he had her at his mercy?

"I'm willing to admit I've never done this," he said, "but with you, I'm more than willing to try."

"That's all I can ask," she replied.

"I should take you here, with you like this." He sighed. "It'd be perfect payback for what happened in my car."

"No apologies."

"None needed, Joss."

She shivered at the sound of her name in his glorious voice. Something she hoped she never got used to.

"However, you've made a request, and I intend to see it through. Roll onto your back, stretch your arms above your head, wrists together."

Trying not to look too eager, she stood and stretched before complying. She finally got to face a disheveled August, who sucked in a breath as she sat on the bed. He'd removed his tie and left the top two buttons of his shirt undone, revealing a swath of porcelain skin flushed with his own desire. With a flick of her tongue over her lips, she scooted back just a bit then lay back the way he'd requested, arms above her head like a sacrifice.

He whispered something in his beautiful language, and, from the heat in his eyes, Joss figured he'd said something dirty. Hoped so, anyway. With the silk pulled taut between his hands, he stalked around the bed, his gaze roaming over her prone form. The pulsing between her thighs became pure torture, but she loved this. Being on stage, where hundreds of lust-clouded eyes watched her strut and shake her ass faded in the light of August's full, rapt attention. He belonged to her, and she belonged to him…. She shivered again at the delight of being his, if only for the night.

Yeah, right. Considering Madame Eve's reputation…. *Stop it. There's a perfect man standing over you, tying you up with an ice-blue silk tie, and you are going to enjoy it.*

She relaxed into the material around her wrists, into the slight strain as August tied the other end to the bedrail. Back slightly arched, she waited for his next move.

Slinking back around the bed, he undid one button at a time, eyes never leaving her face. Any restraint evaporated the moment his shirt hit the floor. The well-defined muscles she'd felt beneath his shirt that first time beckoned for her fingertips, her lips, her tongue. Maybe she hadn't thought the whole tying-up thing all the way through.

Without speaking, he unbuttoned his jeans. Joss pressed her thighs together in a pathetic attempt to alleviate the ache. He pulled the fabric down, revealing his thick, rigid cock and muscular legs. A fresh wave of arousal flooded her.

"You're killing me," she said, her voice more hoarse than normal.

"You've been killing me for days." He kissed her left ankle. "I fantasized about you before I ever saw you." A kiss to her right ankle. "Right here, in this bed." He licked the length of her calf and nipped the back of her knee, spreading her legs along the way. "I dreamed of Natalia Bishop, the woman who belonged to that incredible voice, imagined her on top of me, riding me with the same ferocity she used when she sang." Hovering centimeters above the apex of her thighs, he held her gaze. "That woman is nothing compared to you, Jocelyn." With his thumbs, he spread her lower lips.

"Fuck, August," she whimpered, as he pulled her throbbing clit into his mouth. A breathy moan built in her throat while her orgasm built in her core and crashed into her without warning. Pulling against the restraint, she writhed beneath him, eager to touch him—his mouth on her pussy and his hands cupping her ass were not enough. "I need you. Please."

"You ask so nicely." He disappeared for a moment. Joss heard him rummaging in a drawer, and when he returned, he draped himself over her like a blanket. She hooked a leg around him, urging him to meet her lips. When he crushed his mouth to hers, he eased his cock inside her; her breath hitched, and he kissed her calm again. This was not the frenzied fucking in the car. This was....

Making love.

Making music.

What she wanted forever.

This time, an orgasm bubbled in her, gently pushing her toward the edge. Calm, amazing, perfect. His muscles tensed, his body went rigid, and he clutched the sheets.

"Jocelyn," he bit out.

They rode the wave together. He managed to untie her, and her arms shot around his neck of their own accord, fingers tangling in his hair. They kissed until kisses turned to unspoken promises, and a new melody took root in Joss's mind.

"Stay with me," she whispered.

"Always," he replied. "For you, anything."

She smiled. "What do we do now? About the contract, about you being my boss?"

Pulling her close, he kissed her hair. "We'll deal with whatever comes." He took a deep breath. "I didn't expect you to be my date. When we met, I knew I had to have you, and nothing else mattered. You drew me like music draws me. I dreamed of you that entire night. And with all this.... I firmly believe the company will survive any pitfall our relationship might cause. Micah will handle any negative press, and we will do whatever it takes to help Valkyrie Rysing become a major success."

"You mean that?"

"With all my heart. Passion should be rewarded." Tilting her chin up, he brushed his lips over hers. "And I will ensure yours is."

For the first time in a long time, Joss breathed a sigh of complete relief, the last of the tension leaving her muscles. She curled into August and listened to his heart, the drumbeat of her new favorite song.

About the Author

Catherine Peace has been telling stories for as long as she could remember. She often blames two things for her forays into speculative fiction - Syfy (when it was still SciFi) channel Sundays with her dad and The Island of Dr. Moreau by HG Wells.

She graduated Northern Kentucky University in 2008 and is still chasing the dream of being super rich and famous, mostly so she can sit around in her PJs all day and write stories.

When not being a slave to the people in her her head, she's a slave to two adorable dogs and blogging at:

authorcpeace.com
facebook.com/lexcade
twitter.com/lexcade

Also by Catherine Peace

This Time Next Year
Complete Me
Gemini